THE ELEPHANT TREE

THE ELEPHANT TREE

H. C. LUGER

The Viking Press   New York

First Edition
Copyright © Harriett Mandelay Luger, 1978
All rights reserved
First published in 1978 by The Viking Press
625 Madison Avenue, New York, N.Y. 10022
Published simultaneously in Canada by
Penguin Books Canada Limited
Printed in U.S.A.
1 2 3 4 5 82 81 80 79 78

Library of Congress Cataloging in Publication Data
Luger, H.C.   The elephant tree.

Summary: Lost together in the California desert, two
tough kids from hostile gangs are forced to acknowledge
their mutual dependence.
[1. Survival—Fiction.   2. Deserts—Fiction] I. Title.
PZ7.L97813El   [Fic]   77-16416
ISBN 0-670-29173-0

to Mollie and Leo Mandelay

THE ELEPHANT TREE

ONE

They drove me and five other dudes to the desert
for four days just before Easter. The first time I
saw the other guys was when my old man
dropped me off in front of the County Social
Service Building with my sleeping bag early Monday morning. They were waiting for me—a fat
kid, a black kid in a black knit cap pulled down
over his ears, a redhead, a Mexican, and a guy
about my size. All I knew about them was that

they were ninth graders with a "problem," like me.

I'm Dave Starr. My problem was coming to school once or twice a week. After counseling me and hassling me and warning me all year, the vice principal called me in and told me this was it. The last chance before they sent me over to Juvenile Court. I could cooperate and enroll in this program they were pushing or tell it to the judge. I knew if my mom and my stepfather had to go to court for me, he would beat me up, and she would cry and hit the bottle, so I said I would cooperate.

But I cut out of the first session of the program, where they got acquainted with each other.

During Easter vacation we were going to the big desert near San Diego, not too far from L.A. and a lot of other places you probably never heard of, like San Gregorio, and don't bother. I hardly knew where it was myself until my stepfather got a job at the air base and made us move there. It used to be an old citrus town. The military found it in World War II, and the aircraft plants moved in, and it got big enough to have four high schools.

Anyway, Ray, the black kid, and the guy about my size, whose name was Louie, and me rode in a square red Toyota jeep driven by a college dude named Ted, who was going to be our big brother. The jeep was his. It was brand-new, with covered off-road lights sticking up like Mickey Mouse ears above the windshield.

The three other guys drove in a big station wagon with all the camping gear and Mr. Sloan, who was going to be our father. He and Ted were supposed to rap with us every week and take us to ball games and on trips and like that. This desert trip was the kickoff. It was a big deal.

Ray sat in front with Ted, giving him a line, and Louie and I faced each other on the little seats against the sides of the car in back. We looked each other over. Like I said, we were about evenly matched, not small, not tall. He had dark hair like mine, but his eyes were blue in a pale, ugly, sort of shrunk-up face. He chewed on the middle fingernail of his right hand, while those little red-rimmed eyes traveled over every inch of me.

"Where you from?" I asked.

"Barber. You?"

"Jefferson."

I knew we were enemies. Sam Barber High is the nearest high school to Jefferson. Over a year ago, before I came to Jefferson, two Barbers got beat up by some Jays near the boundary of the two districts—I don't know why, and I couldn't care less. Then the Barbers beat up a few Jays. Then guys from the two schools started cruising through each other's turf, you know, like a challenge, and a Jay claimed Barbers slashed his tires. Then the cops got involved, and the whole hassle began to cool off a little, but Jays and Barbers traded insults whenever they met. So I waited.

"Jays eat dirt for Barbers," Louie said.

"Up yours," I said, and I waited some more. Louie tried to stare me down, but I did not blink, even though my eyeballs got dry.

Louie took his knife from his pocket and with a

flick of his wrist held it open, low, where Ted could not see it in the rear-view mirror. "Know what makes a good Barber? A sharp blade." He honed it back and forth on his palm and tested the edge with a finger. I pretended to clean my fingernails with my Buck knife. Then I sat with it between my knees, pointed at him.

Because this is the way I am. If a guy starts up with me, *he* has to be the one to back away.

"Hey, Dave, Louie, what's your sport? Football, baseball?" Ted gave us a quick grin over his shoulder.

"Fighting," Louie said, looking at me.

"Be serious," Ted said, grinning at us in the mirror.

"We are, we are!" I said.

"They call me killer," Louie said.

"O.K. I'll take you two killers down to the gym and we'll see what you can do," Ted said, and changed the subject because he didn't really want to hear about us guys. He wanted to brag about the jeep—the winch and grille guard sitting on the front bumper, the sand tires that had cost sixty dollars apiece, the red-spoke wheels, double-roll bars, headers. "I got a bundle in this baby," he said, stroking the seat between him and Ray as if he was stroking a girl. Only the CB radio failed him. It was totally dead. He figured it had a short, and he was going to take it back to the dealer as soon as he got back to town.

Louie and I put our blades in our pockets and jived with Ted and Ray and watched each other all the way to the desert.

We arrived at the campground in the afternoon, and it was hot. Right away I knew camping was not my thing. An empty vacant lot, glary in the sunlight, stretched for miles in all directions. Crowded in the middle of it were some trailers, a few tents, campers, motor homes, the Ranger's office, and a building with the head and showers.

That was it. Nothing else, except a dry wind whipping the bushes and blowing up sand.

Pop (Mr. Sloan told us to call him Pop) and Ted helped us set up our pup tents and unpack the gear. There were two campsites right next to each other, each with a fire pit and long table with benches attached to it. Louie was with Ted and Ray and the redhead in the other campsite. The Chicano and the fat kid and me had our tents with Pop.

It took us about an hour and a half to get squared away, and when we finished, Pop had hamburgers ready. We ate, four on a side, at one of the tables. While I ate, I finally got the guys' names and faces straight in my mind. Mike, the redhead, sat across from me on the end. He looked like a Huck Finn, straight out of Disney. He came from Kennedy High across town. Next to him was the fat kid, whose name was Tony. He was also from Kennedy. He didn't talk. At first I thought he was deaf. When Louie, who sat next to him, started calling him Two-Ton Tony and punching him on the arm, and Tony just sat there, not smiling, not frowning, not telling Louie to go to hell or kiss my butt, I wondered if he was retarded. Big Brother Ted sat on the other side of Louie at the far end of the table. I got a better look at him. He was the beefy blond fullback type who acted like he had it made.

Ray sat across the table from Ted. He was small and very black. He was from Roosevelt. He ran with the Black Berets. Pop sat next to him, and between Pop and me was Joe, the Chicano. He was tall and thin, and almost had a mustache.

"Hey, man, did you ever see so much empty?" he asked me as we ate.

"I have never seen so much *nothing*!" I said.

"Where you from?"

"Bradley High. Segundos," he said. The Segundos were a Chicano gang from around Second Street.

Joe and I watched a man in the camping space next to ours unchain a Honda from the bumper of his camper truck and ride away on a dirt road that went from the campground straight out to nowhere.

"Man, would I like to be on that," Joe said.

"If I had one of those things to ride, I might even like it here," I said.

"You ain't kidding," Joe said. "You come down in the jeep with Ray and Louie?"

I nodded.

"They cool?"

I shrugged. Why should I tell him anything? The sun went down, and right away it was cold. The man on the Honda came back. He was old and had a beer belly. He was pleased with himself, you could tell. I wished I had that little Honda.

When it got dark, the people went to a show. We had to go, too. Near the Ranger's office was a place with rows of logs flattened on top to sit on, and a fire in a round fire pit down in front to look at. We sat in a row on a log at the back like Boy Scouts while Pop and Ted went to the Ranger's office to find out about trails and get maps. Louie went in first and sat on one end, chewing on his fingernails. I was the last one in, and I sat at the other end of the row. We told each other what a drag this camping trip was going to be.

"My woman is going to miss me," Mike said.

Joe said, "I got a dozen women, and the ugliest one looks like Miss America from here."

"No women, no liquor, no grass—" Mike said.

"I got grass," Ray said, "fifty cents a hit."

"What do you want to do, get rich off your friends?" I asked.

"You my friends?" Ray asked. "What did you guys ever do for me?"

"We're in the same boat with you," I said. "We're like shipwrecked together."

"Worse," Joe said. "If you're shipwrecked you can swim around. What're we going to do around here for four days?"

"You better clean up Number Two campsite. It stinks," Louie said.

"What do you mean, Number Two campsite. We are *Número Uno*!" Joe said.

Louie answered Joe but looked straight at me. "With Slobbo and that garbage pig Dave for bunkmates, your luck sure ran out this trip!" he said deliberately. "You're the only man there!"

The other guys came alive, looking back and forth from him to me. The only one who was completely out of it was Tony, who sat between Louie and Mike like a lump of unbaked dough.

I boiled. "Listen, craphead, shut your face, or

I'll shove your own stink right down your throat!" The other guys brightened up and began to shine, but before anything more could be said, Ted and Pop sat down next to me.

The show started. The Ranger gave us a few jokes, led a few songs, told us the rules for using the desert, and then laid the big number of the evening on us—*a slide show!* One after another, thrilling pictures of rocks, cactus, lizards, and flowers flashed on the screen. *Wow!*

"Now I am going to show you the rare and famous elephant tree that bleeds when it is cut. No one knows for sure how old this specimen is, but it could be a hundred years old, an excellent example of the slow growth of desert plants. . . ."

It did not look like an elephant, and it did not look like a tree, and who cared?

Suddenly everybody except us guys was singing "Goodnight, Ladies," and the show was over. We went to our tents and hit the sack. I lay there in the dark, thinking of one of the slides we had seen. It was a close-up of the head of a rattlesnake, its mouth open wide, its fangs curved backwards to give you a better shot of venom. The eyes were bright, hateful, watchful. It reminded me of Louie.

TWO

The next morning when I crawled out of the pup tent, I saw first the miles and miles of vacant lot surrounding the camp, sunny, empty, then Pop making a fire in the crumbling fire pit that came with the campsite. Ted and the jeep were gone.

Pop did all the cooking over an open fire. He piled the wood just so, and as he fanned the little starter flame, he talked to it. When it caught, he shouted, "Right on!" grinning at me as if it was a big deal. I thought he was crazy, but, man, could he cook! The beautiful smell of bacon filled the bright, glary morning, and the guys crawled out of their sacks ready to eat.

Ted roared in just as we were sitting down to breakfast, the shining red jeep covered with dust.

"You should have seen where I went!" he yelled as he jumped down. "Pop, you guys, wait till I show you what she can do!"

After we ate, Mike and Ray and me got in the jeep with Ted. We took off down the highway till we came to a road marked FOUR-WHEEL-DRIVE VEHICLES ONLY, and we turned onto it. Man, what a trip! All I could do was hang on and brace myself and yell and laugh as I bounced and jerked and slid and slammed.

We bumped over rocks as big as horses. We fell into ruts. Sometimes we tipped higher on one side than the other. Then we came to a place of deep sand, and the wheels sank, and I thought we were stuck, but the old jeep ground her teeth and pulled us through with no effort. We tilted back on our rear wheels and climbed a hill that went straight up. Man, what a trip! All the time Ted was bragging up his car.

We arrived at another smooth road and pulled up in a turnout to wait for the station wagon. We would change places with the other guys going back so they would have a chance to ride in the jeep. Ted worried about Pop. He was afraid there would be no chance for him to take a ride, because he was always busy.

In a few minutes the station wagon pulled up beside us, and we started on the three-thousand-mile hike they had planned for us that Tuesday. My feet started to hurt in about ten minutes. What a drag! "Get the jeep!" I yelled, and Ray and Louie took it up, and then the others. Nothing to see except bushes and rocks and dirt, the sun beating my back like a whip, and the sweat rolling off my face and down my neck. The guys stopped every few yards for a drink from canteens we had snapped on army belts around our waists.

"What's keeping you guys? Get the lead out!" Ted yelled at us from up ahead.

"It's hot, man!" I yelled back. "Get the jeep!"

"You call this hot?" Pop laughed, waiting for us to catch up. "It isn't even eighty today. I've been here, right on this trail, when it was almost a hundred."

"He's crazy," I said to Joe.

"You ain't kidding!" Joe said.

Pop gave each of us a friendly slap on the shoulder or butt as we passed. "Watch out for rattlers, fellas. Don't step on 'em, don't sit on 'em!" He laughed again. Big joke.

"Snakes?" Louie said, and he kind of wilted. He started gnawing on his thumbnail.

"That old man *is* crazy," I said to Joe. "I wonder if he's safe."

"We'll be lucky to get back to town alive," Joe said, looking gloomy.

We climbed sharply along the side of a hill. Ted started singing and hamming it up like an opera singer. The son-of-a-bitch could climb hills and sing at the same time. He wasn't even sweating. I looked at the calves bulging out of his hiking boots, and the neck and shoulders like a

18

bull's, and I hated the guy.

The trail went over big boulders, and as we climbed we got hotter and sweatier and meaner. Ted had to cut his act short and shove his big jock body between guys punching and cussing, to keep them from hurting each other.

Only Tony had nothing to say. He kept to himself, pulling himself over rocks, lowering himself carefully, melting and dripping in the sun, completely closed and silent.

After about five years of torture we came to a little gully with small, scraggly trees growing from its banks, a few flowers here and there, and patches of plants growing flat on the ground.

"Here we are," Pop said. "This is it." We guys plopped down in the shade of the little trees— everybody except Louie.

"What about snakes?" he asked, peering into the twisted roots.

"Well, look around before you sit," Pop said. Louie found a piece of dried root and poked behind and under rocks and among the trunks and stems of the trees and bushes. Then he sat down in the center of the gully, where he could watch for snakes.

Pop scored again with lunch. He had a way with a plain old cheese sandwich like no one else I ever knew. He was a real chow artist. And we had tomatoes and fruit and cookies. Some of the guys were running out of water.

"I told you fellas to ration your water," Pop said, and it was true, he had, but no one had paid any attention.

After lunch we lay around eating our oranges and looking at the sky. The gully was almost pretty compared to what was around it. Pop wasn't a bad old guy, and he sure was a good cook. It didn't cost anything to make him happy, so I said, "Man, I never knew the desert was so neat."

Pop beamed at me.

"Yeh, man, what are all those squatty, dusty bushes with little bittie gray leaves?" Louie asked, winking at the guys.

He had eaten, he was rested, he felt better. Now he had to mock me. I got the message loud and clear. So did the other guys. They watched us with interest.

"Saltbush. Why do you want to know?"

"They're fascinating," Louie smirked. "And these crooked bare stems with the leaves hanging in bunches?"

The guys snickered.

"Creosote bush—"

"I saw an elephant tree, Pop," I said, to one-up Louie.

"You're putting me on, fella. They don't grow around here." Pop smiled at Ted, who was lying on his back, staring up at the clouds. "How about this bunch of nature fakers, Ted?"

"Baby bullthrowers," Ted said dreamily. "You can tell by their ears." So damn cute. Made you want to puke.

But it was peaceful there. Hot and quiet and peaceful. No one spoke for a few minutes.

"Any of you boys done much camping?" Pop asked.

"I used to go all the time before my old man got wasted in Vietnam," Mike said. "I've been camping all over this country. My old man was in the Air Force, and we lived in Texas and Colorado and Mississippi. We'd jump in the car and take off whenever we had time. It was bitchin'!" Mike's voice faded away, and he looked out across the desert. I could tell he was remembering.

Louie wanted to play games some more. "Hey, man, look at that big bird flying over us! I bet it's an eagle!"

"Buzzard," Ted said.

"You sure? Man, look at the size of it!"

"Buzzard," said Ted, shielding his eyes from the sun to look at it.

"Come on, man, look at how it glides!" Louie squinted up at the bird overhead, sliding on the air, circling, dipping its wings now and then to keep steady. "You going to tell me that's nothing but a buzzard? That bird's got too much class to be a buzzard!"

"Buzzard, looking for carrion," Ted said, still lying on his back and watching the bird as it sat on the air, slowly turning.

"Looking for what?" Joe asked.

"Dead flesh," Ted said.

"I hate buzzards," Ray said, not looking up. "They're bad luck."

"Don't believe that garbage. You're too smart for that. Buzzards have a bad name because they eat dead flesh."

"That's what I mean! Who wants to be dead?"

"That's not the point—"

Ray interrupted. "Sure it's the point, man! Find me a rabbit or a cow that will lay down and say, 'Come on to dinner, buzzard baby'!"

"You want all that dead stuff lying around, crawling with maggots, stinking up the place?" Ted asked, still smiling. That son-of-a-bitch would never be dead, I thought. His kind lives forever.

"Suppose *you're* what's dirtyin' up the place and smellin' bad. That means you're dead, man, and I'd say that's bad luck."

"I'd say that's the worst luck," Louie said.

"Suppose you were dead, man," Ray insisted.

Ted shook his head. "That's not the point."

Pop cut in. "Let's change the subject. Tony, tell us about yourself. You ever been camping?"

Tony looked at him in his dumb, closed-up way, but he didn't say a word.

"Hey, Two-Ton, how come you talk so much?" Louie said, sinking his fist in Tony's big belly.

"His tongue is too fat, he can't move it. Show us your tongue, Two-Ton!" said Joe.

"You fat all over? Show us what you got, Tony!" Louie said.

Tony struggled to his feet and moved away to lower himself carefully on a rock apart from the group but close enough to hear what was going on.

"*Knock it off!*" Pop was not smiling. "I don't see anybody around here who looks better than anyone else. We're here to help each other. Understand?"

We wiped the grins off and put on serious faces, and for an hour or so we had to talk about our problems.

Mike came to school drunk. "A couple times I got carried away. I just forgot to stop." He grinned. "I like it, especially sweet wine. Listen, man, I can handle it, only once in a while I have a bad day, and like I say, I forget to stop. . . ."

Joe got caught spray-painting his gang's *placa* on a freeway overpass "to show we're here, man!"

"To show who?" Pop asked.

"*Ríos.* The ones by the river."

Mike snorted. "They don't know?"

"It don't hurt to advertise."

"How come you Chicanos don't stick together instead of splitting into gangs and trying to kill each other?" Ted asked. He sounded like a tourist visiting Mexico.

Joe got excited. "We're not a gang! The *Ríos,* that's a gang. Us, we are like cousins . . . !"

Pop shook his head. "Ray, what's your problem?"

"I don't know any problem, unless it's my straight-F average, and that don't bother me none."

"You want to stay in the ghetto all your life? Don't you want to *get someplace?*" Ted asked. They sat side by side—big blond Ted with his clear skin and friendly smiles; Ray about half his size, very dark, with the dusty black watch cap pulled down over his ears, the poker face giving nothing.

"Where you want me to get to?" he asked.

Pop said my name. I told how I cut out of school because all my friends are at Rancho Verde High, where I would have gone if my step-father hadn't made us move to San Gregorio. "I would have dug Rancho Verde," I said. "I wouldn't have cut out there."

"We'll have to find out why you haven't made friends in seven months," Pop said. "Louie?"

"I'm a troublemaker," he said, sneering at Pop. "That's what they call me, because I don't take no crap from nobody. Not guys, not teachers, not anyone. I'm just not having any." He stared at Pop without smiling.

"Even when no crap is intended?" Pop said mildly, ignoring the challenge.

"I can smell it a mile away," Louie said, looking at me.

Then it was Tony's turn, again, but he turned

26

around on his rock and gave us his big backside. He had been listening with his mouth open, his eyes, sunk deep into his cheeks, darting from speaker to speaker. Pop let us know Tony had done a little bit of shoplifting.

Finally Pop made a speech, telling us that we would be exploring ourselves and our problems in the weeks to come, and that he would like to see friendships develop among us. "I hope you fellas will feel that you can trust Ted and me," he ended up. "We want to help you."

"I bet they get paid plenty," Joe whispered to me.

I nodded. I didn't really care. Maybe they had nothing better to do with their time. Maybe messing around in other people's business turned them on. Or maybe they *were* getting rich, like Joe said. I didn't give a damn. I just wanted the next two days to pass as quickly as possible.

Then we started back. It was even harder going down than coming up. We were tired, and in addition to having to climb over the big rocks again, we slipped and slid on the downhill trail.

My calf and thigh muscles ached from bracing myself. I'd had enough for one day, but there was no way to quit. My own two legs had to get me back to the cars. On top of everything else, I ran out of water. By this time no one except Pop and Ted had any left.

"Teach you a lesson," Pop said cheerfully. "Tomorrow you'll ration yourself better." I began to hate him almost as much as I hated Ted.

"*No way* I'm going to do this crap again tomorrow!" Ray said.

Louie and I found ourselves next to each other. "Get away from me, garbage pig!" he said. I let him have it, hard, on the arm, and he pivoted and threw a left hook at me. Ted was between us.

"You guys got a problem?" he asked, smiling that friendly, sunny smile. We dropped our arms.

"Screw you!" Louie said to Ted between his teeth, but Ted kept smiling down at us from his cloud next to God until we turned away and started walking.

The path narrowed as it went between two

boulders, and there was room for only one guy at a time. Louie and I were still next to each other, and we reached the narrow place together. I started through, but Louie slammed me against the rock so he could go first. I shoved him, and he fell. I had my fists up, but when he jumped up, he ran away screaming.

"Oh, my God! I been bit! Rattlesnake!"

We cleared out. I mean we *flew* away from that boulder, even Two-Ton Tony. He jumped as high and as far and as fast as anybody else. Ted tackled Louie and held him in a bear hug, telling him to be still, the worst thing he could do was move around. Louie fought Ted as long as his strength lasted, yelling and hollering.

Meantime, Pop inspected the area where Louie fell. "There's no snake," he said. "There's some cholla cactus, and he probably got a glimpse of this." He held up a twisted, dried piece of wood. One end curved up, and if you were scared enough, you could make a snake's head out of it. Louie was scared enough. He sat huddled next to Ted, chewing on his nails, shaking.

"You're O.K., fella," Pop told him. "You just fell into some cholla cactus." He held out his canteen. Louie was shaking so, he slopped the water all over himself as he tried to drink. When he handed back the canteen, Pop told him to take off his pants and give them to Ted, so he could pick out the stickers, and then to lie down on his stomach. Louie was not breathing so hard now, and his color was coming back. The rest of us guys leaned against the boulder smirking and watching Pop pull cactus spines out of Louie's bare butt. I picked up the twisted stick.

"Bit in the ass by a wood snake," I said, and the other guys took up the chant. "Bit in the ass by a wood snake!" they jeered.

Suddenly Tony laughed, a high, girlish giggle. Louie sprang up at him and punched him in the stomach, in the face, on the head, as if Tony was a punching bag. Tony dropped to the ground and curled up like a cocoon. Pop and Ted hung on to Louie, but he still tried to kick Tony. Finally Louie was quiet, and Pop went over to Two-Ton, who was still lying on the ground, his fat arms over his face, snuffling like a baby. Pop helped him to his feet and checked him over. Pop told Louie to put on his pants, and then we started down the trail again.

Poor old blubbering Tony stumbled along between me and Pop, while Louie had to walk next to Ted. There was not much talking. It was about all we could do to put one foot in front of the other. All we thought about was getting back to the cars and taking the load off our tired feet. But I couldn't resist saying just loud enough for everyone to hear, "Bit in the ass . . ." and I snickered.

"I'll kill you!" Louie choked. Ted grabbed him.

"Knock it off, Dave!" Pop said, and he meant it.

Twenty years later we were back to the cars. Ray and Louie and I collapsed into the station wagon and rode to camp totally bushed.

THREE

Tony crawled into his tent, but the rest of us just dropped on the ground and conked out while Pop got a fire going, set a pot of beans on the grate, cut up onions, pickles, and tomatoes, and then we roasted hot dogs. Tony appeared without being called. After dinner Pop went to hunt up the Ranger again, and Ted wandered over to a campsite where he had seen a couple women without guys.

We sat around, waiting for Tuesday to be over. We were still bushed from the hike and too full from eating to do much except yawn a lot and stretch. The old dude on the Honda came putt-putting back from the desert with his fat old wife behind him. We talked about what we would do if we had that bike. Then we talked about the jeep, and how we would rather ride around in four-wheel-drive than knock ourselves out on the damn hills and rocks.

"And you wouldn't get bit in the ass by a wood snake," I said. The guys laughed and hooted, and Louie cursed me. Then he reached into his pocket. I thought he was going for his blade, and my hand went into my pocket.

"Who wants to go for a ride in the jeep?" Louie asked, holding up some small thing instead. It was an ignition key. "Let's go ride in the jeep."

"How did you get that key?" Ray asked.

"Big Brother Ted lost it."

"Where?"

"In the ignition." Now the guys were laughing *with* Louie. "When I give it back, he'll owe me a big favor, right? The stupid jock, suppose it got into the wrong hands?" Everybody but me cracked up. Louie looked at me. "What's the matter, Davie baby, don't you have no sense of humor?"

"You're not going anywhere. You don't know how to drive a four-wheel-drive."

"Watch me."

"How are you going to get away without letting the whole campground know about it?"

Louie grinned. "When the music lovers sing their song, I split."

The guys almost killed themselves laughing. "All *right*!" they yelled. "Way to go!"

Mike said, "Cool it!" as Ted and a woman passed us on their way to the jeep. They climbed in, and we watched, snickering and laughing. In a minute Ted stuck his head out and called over to us, putting on the Big Man act for the woman.

"Any of you dudes been fooling around with my car?" We shook our heads. "Did any of you jokers happen to see my key?"

"Did you lose it, Ted?" Louie asked as we all moved toward the jeep.

"I would have sworn I left it in the ignition," Ted said.

We helped him look under the car and all around. The woman got out, and we looked under the seat and pulled back the floor mat. Finally Ted said, "Forget it. I have another one hidden in the chassis. I'm always losing my keys. Usually I lose the whole schmear, but this time I got smart and left my ring at home . . . but I *know* I left it in the ignition."

We stood around while he went through his pockets and his wallet one more time. Then he said, "Forget it," and he took his extra key from wherever he kept it and drove off with the woman. It really was a crack-up, I had to admit.

"Who's coming?" Louie said when we stopped laughing.

"Two-Ton Tony," Mike said. Tony took a step backward, flinging up his arm to protect his face.

"He's too fat. He'll slow me down. I got to make a quick move. Who's coming?"

Tony lowered his arm and went back to hanging on every word with his mouth open.

Ray said, "Your friend Dave wants to come with you."

"Screw you!" I said to Ray.

"No way I'm taking that garbage pig. I'm not driving no garbage truck!"

"Dave, you gonna take that shit?" Ray asked. "I'm tired of hearing him put you down that way!"

"Show him up, man! Go with him! He's afraid of you!" Joe said.

"Why can't he go by himself? Maybe he's scared!" I said.

"A garbage pig like you wouldn't understand. I'm a sociable guy. I'm not selfish. I want to share! Mike, you coming? Ray? Joe?"

"Dave insists," Mike said.

"No *way!*" I said.

"What's the matter, you dudes afraid to be alone together?" Ray asked. I flashed on Louie in the jeep honing his knife on his palm.

"I keep telling you, it's the stink!" Louie said.

Ray lifted his nose and sniffed. He nodded. "I do smell something." He pretended to recognize the smell. "It's chicken shit, that's what it is, and they both smell of it!"

"Here, chick, chick, chick!" Joe stretched his neck, flapped his arms, and crowed like a rooster. "You girls need a big daddy to take care of you?" And he crowed again. Louie was chewing his fingernails and watching me with eyes like that rattler's I had seen the night before.

"When?" I said.

"You'll know," he said.

Just then Pop appeared. "O.K., fellas, let's go to the show." We followed him and once again sat on the log like Boy Scouts. A little later Ted hurried up to our log and sat down.

A different Ranger gave the jokes and the songs and the same old rules for the desert.

"Take water."

"Vehicles must stay on the roads at all times."

"Get out of the narrow canyons if it starts to rain."

Then he showed slides about rocks and hills. I

did not see anything. I did not hear a word. I thought about what I would do with Louie. A lot depended on him, but I knew I had to come on strong. I was not sure I could take him, but if I showed weakness, he would be all over me. I was scared.

I sat between Mike and Joe, and they poked me and looked at Louie, who sat chewing his nails between Ray and Mike, getting the same business from them. When the Ranger had been yakking for a long time, Louie got up and stepped hard on my foot on his way out. After about five minutes Joe whispered, "Good luck, killer."

I got up. Pop looked at me, and I pointed to the head.

"Find Louie," he whispered, and I nodded.

I found Louie. He was waiting for me.

Without a word we walked to our campsites where the high red jeep sat waiting for us. We got in. The singing broke out. Louie turned the ignition key, the motor caught, Louie shifted gears, and we roared off into the desert. While the campers sat on logs and sang "I'll See You in My Dreams," the jeep scampered into the great big empty.

FOUR

"I'll see you in my dreams!"

Louie and I bounced along the dirt road, singing and hollering like crazy. I felt as if a valve had popped inside of me and the pressure was off. I was high, dipping and rocking in the square little car, looking out over the blunt, wide hood, yelling my head off. For a few minutes Louie and I were not enemies. Not friends, but not enemies.

Suddenly Louie veered off the dirt road and, still yelling at the top of his lungs, cut across country, steering in crazy curves, circles, figure eights. I was slammed against the door, against the dash, against him. Outside the car the scene was like a planet in outer space—bare ground, bare hills, rocks, gullies, ugly bushes sitting lonely, the moon, low in the sky, staring at us through the car window. I was scared. I punched Louie on the arm.

"Hey, man, where we going?"

"Let's take a little ride before I and you settle up. Maybe we can dope something out so neither of us gets hurt."

"How we gonna get back?"

"Scared, chickie?"

"There aren't any street signs out here, you ass!"

"Ever hear of the stars, chickie? Look, there's the moon. Now it's in our right hand. When we want to go back, we keep it in our left hand, like sailors, see?" He started singing again, and again I punched him.

"You are full of it, man! Get back on the jeep road before you lose our butt!"

Louie stopped singing. He was Ugly Louie again. "This is my party, craphead! You don't like it—get out!" He floored the gas pedal, and we headed for a boulder towering ahead of us, black against a black sky. I braced myself for the crash, but at the last moment he swerved, and I was thrown against the window, then cracked my skull on the windshield as the engine stalled.

I shook my head to clear my mind and felt my forehead for blood, but there was none. The windshield was not even cracked. I was beginning to get a headache. I turned to Louie, who had apparently got the steering wheel in his gut because he was holding his stomach and looking as if he was trying not to cry. When he saw me looking at him, he straightened up and turned the ignition key. The engine caught right away, but when he shifted to reverse, it roared and whined and stalled. He tried again. And again.

"What kind of lousy four-wheel-drive is this?" he said.

"I thought you knew how to drive a four-wheel-drive."

"I do. There's something wrong with this one."

"There was nothing wrong with it today when Ted drove it," I said.

Louie tried every gear again and again. The engine roared and whined and stalled. Louie's face got pinched and wrinkled.

"You broke it, you ass," I said.

"We'll have to dig ourselves out," he said in a shaky voice. "Maybe the four-wheel-drive went out." He started chewing his nails.

I found a shovel under the front seat and began digging. Louie, using his hands, scooped sand from behind the other front wheel. I forgot about my headache as I dug behind first the front, then the rear wheel on the passenger side of the car. When we had made a kind of dent behind each tire, Louie got in and tried again.

"Hey, you're going in deeper!" I yelled before the engine stalled. Then I had a thought. "You sure you got her in four-wheel-drive?"

"Sure I got it in four-wheel-drive! What do you

think I am—stupid like you?" He tried a few more times. No luck. He got out of the car and lighted a cigarette. I climbed behind the wheel. I had never driven a four-wheel-drive, and all I knew to do was to try all the gears, but of course nothing happened.

"I never drove one that acted like this before," Louie said.

"You wrecked it, big man," I said, getting out and fishing my smokes from my pocket. I was cold and tired and scared. I lighted up and looked around.

Chunks of blackness darker than the night surrounded us. I knew they were only rocks and bushes, but we were on their territory, and they were threatening us. . . . It was Louie's fault. *He* had ripped off the ignition key. *He* left the jeep road and took off cross-country. *He* wrecked the goddamn car and got us stuck out here miles from the goddamn camp . . . and no one knows where we are . . . *no one knows where we are . . .* NO ONE KNOWS WHERE WE ARE! I looked up into the sky to find the moon.

My God!

A million lights hung in the sky! Big lights, little lights, bright lights that sparkled, dim lights you could hardly see, faint clouds of light—all surrounded by black emptiness so huge, so deep. . . .

In the city I see fifty stars, and I say, "Wow, what a clear night!"

Here I saw a million stars hanging over my head with space for every one of them . . . around those lights, behind those lights, black space as still, as cold . . . as death.

Maybe the earth is lost in space the way I am lost in the desert. . . .

And the moon! Where is the moon?

"Where's the moon?" I screamed at Louie, and I heard my tiny, high-pitched voice running away to outer space, to the end of time, to death. . . . "You stupid ass, we lost the moon! *Now* how are we going to get back?"

"Watch yourself, chickie. Watch who you call a stupid ass." He had on his Ugly Louie face, but I could see by his eyes that he was terrified.

"You stupid, *stupid* ass! First you get off the road, then you wreck the car! Now you lose the moon! You stupid ass!"

Louie rushed me, throwing a punch at my chin, but I blocked it with my shoulder and landed one in his belly. That slowed him down, and I stepped away. All of a sudden I did not want to waste time fighting. I wanted to get the hell back to camp.

"We better cool it," I said. "We have to get our ass back to camp." Louie did not follow up.

"O.K., later," he said. "Don't think I'll forget this. I'll take care of you later. . . . Let's split."

I looked all around. I could see no clue in that endless dim landscape to show us where to go, and a warning of the Ranger's came into my mind.

"Maybe we better wait here by the jeep till they find us, like the Ranger said."

"No way! I gotta move. This place freaks me out." I knew what he meant. I was glad he wanted to split. "We can follow our tracks back to the jeep road. Then we turn left."

46

"I wonder how far we've come," I said, staring into the dark.

"Not far."

Louie led and I followed. It was just barely possible to make out the ruts dug by the tires in the soft sand. We smoked up all the cigarettes we had, one after another. They tasted like dry straw, but we could not stop smoking. We were cold. We had no sweaters or windbreakers, only our long-sleeved shirts. I kept my eyes on the wheel ruts I could barely see in the sand. If I looked up at the freaky lights in the death-black sky, I panicked; if I looked at the dark shapes we passed in the desert, I panicked. My legs were the only parts of me that were awake. The rest of me was asleep, having a nightmare.

After we had been walking a year or so, Louie slowed and stopped.

"I've lost the goddamn tracks," he said.

We had come out of soft sand onto hard-packed ground, and there was no way we could see the tread marks in the dark. We wandered around looking for soft sand, for a place where the jeep had broken through the crust, for a bush knocked down—any clue. We made bigger and bigger circles. We found soft sand but no tire ruts. Then we could not find the hard-packed ground again. We stopped to look around, for we had been keeping our eyes down, looking for the goddamn tire ruts.

"Hey, man, look over there! Something's happening!" Louie pointed to a glow behind a hill. "Maybe that's the lights of the camp! Maybe there's a town!" We ran to the hill and quickly climbed to the top.

There was nothing happening. There was no camp. There was no town. There was only the great big empty all around, and one edge of it was silver.

"It's the goddamn sun!"

"Look what you've done! We're lost! We should have waited by the car!" I pounded Louie with my fists. He kind of slumped to the ground and didn't get up.

"I won't forget," he half panted, half sobbed from the ground. "You'll get yours later. Just wait till I get my breath back!"

My legs buckled under me. They were so tired they would not hold me. But I was not sleepy. I shivered from rage and panic, and I wouldn't close my eyes because I was afraid Louie would cut my throat if I didn't watch him.

Then I heard him breathing great, tired breaths, in and out, in and out, and I knew he was beyond hurting a fly. I decided to split that very minute. I needed Louie like I needed poison. He was bad luck. I would be better off alone.

I looked around. The endless desert, turning gray, offered no clue as to which direction I should take to get back to camp. While I was trying to make up my mind which way to go, I fell asleep.

FIVE

I sat up, my heart pounding like a fist against my ribs. I did not know where I was. The sun glared on bright sand, on ugly bushes, on a few blue mountains miles away.

Louie was screaming. He sat straight as a board in the bright light, yelling his head off. I remembered where I was.

"What's wrong?" I said. He stopped screaming and stared at me. His eyes seemed to focus.

"I had a nightmare. I dreamed I was lost in the desert and a rattlesnake *this long* was crawling over my face and around my neck. . . . Oh, God, I feel terrible!" He put his head on his knees. I looked at him, bent over and miserable, and I wanted to murder him.

"Hey, killer, let's go! There's the sun! But maybe it'll burn your hand. Maybe we should wait for the moon so you can carry it in one hand, then the other, then lose it!"

"Don't, Dave," Louie said without raising his head. "I feel terrible."

"The poor little craphead feels bad," I mocked him. Then I screamed, "Look what you've done to us, you son-of-a-bitch! I ought to kick your head off!" But I did not move. Louie cried and chewed his nails, one after another.

We sat on that hill for a long time. I had a splitting headache from where I had hit the windshield. My leg muscles ached from hiking, and my back from sleeping on the ground. Since it was only the end of March, the morning was not too hot. What bothered me was the glare.

There was no shade. The sun glared down on us, the desert glared back at us. Every hill, every bush, every rock was harsh and bright and cut into my aching head with a sharp knife edge.

And no one knew where we were.

At that thought my heart would jump and send the blood to my head with the pain of an ax blow.

Finally Louie whined, "I can't sit here any longer. I gotta move!" He stood and surveyed the scene. From the top of our small rise we saw only miles and miles of bushes. "If the sun came up over there—we have to go this way—" He waved his arm. I knew he didn't know from crap, but when he stumped down the hill, I followed.

We staggered across dry ditches we didn't see until we were right on them, through sand that sometimes suddenly sucked at our feet, over rocks that came out of nowhere to block our way. The sun got stronger, the air hotter. My mouth was dry. I took off my jeans and my blue-and-red-plaid shirt, and Louie got out of his clothes, too. His shirt was orange-and-green plaid, but inside of five minutes our bright-colored shirts were the color of dust from being dragged on the ground.

We walked without stopping. Why stop? Where could we sit? In the worthless patches of ragged shadow made by the bushes and runty trees? Louie was afraid of snakes, and besides we could bear our panic better if we moved. We didn't talk. What was there to talk about? We wanted to be found. Then we'd start talking again.

Hours after we left the hill Louie yelled, "Hey, look! A town!"

I followed his outstretched arm, and at first I could not believe what I saw—buildings shimmering in the distance, a lot of them! But they did not look quite right—too watery, too unsubstantial. I shook my head.

"It's a mirage."

"What's the matter, you sore you didn't see it first? It's *there,* man! I even see the roofs of the buildings!"

I followed him as he headed for the town, and kept following him until it disappeared in cracks, the bushes and rocks showing in between. Finally there was only desert meeting sky once again, the bottom and top of an endless box of glare with us trapped in the middle.

We staggered on, following a broad, dry creek bed because it was easier walking. It narrowed and deepened and became rockier, and when the sun was almost overhead, we found ourselves at the mouth of a small canyon in some dry hills or low mountains dotted with dark, shiny rocks and a few bushes. A big one growing on a little mound in the gully blocked our way. We scrambled around it.

Behind the bush the gully narrowed still more. On the right a sandy cut with plants clinging to it here and there rose steeply. Opposite, across the small ravine, a boulder was lodged in the hill, jutting over the bed of the narrow canyon, making a shallow cave about four feet high and deep enough for both of us.

I dove into it, thinking only of getting my burning shoulders in the shade and resting my eyes from the desert glare. Louie waited for me to be bitten by a rattler before he cautiously crawled in after me.

My muscles relaxed, my mind let go, and I slept. It seemed like only a minute, but it must have been an hour or so later that a familiar *chop-chop-chop* shook the air, and I was wide awake. Louie and I scrambled out from under the rock, waving our arms and screaming. A helicopter drifted over the hill and headed slowly away from us.

Yelling and straining with all our strength, we sprinted after it, but slowly as it seemed to move, it quickly left us behind. It got smaller and smaller till it looked like a bug in the sky. Then it disappeared, leaving the canyon, the hills, the sunny sky emptier and quieter than they had been before it came. The only sound besides our panting breaths was the buzzing of a few flies and bees. Louie took off toward the cave, then stopped dead. I knew what stopped him. Snakes.

"Get our clothes, and let's split," he said.

"To where?"

"To where the chopper went. Now we know

which way to go."

"You're crazy."

"Come on, stupid! The sun is on our left now, same as the moon was last night. The chopper is headed the way we came from last night!" Louie was having a fit. He was jumping around and waving his arms, trying to make me get those clothes. There was no way I would leave this place and follow him from one bush to another, one gully to the next, my tongue dry in my mouth, my skin burning. My shoulders were beginning to blister.

"I'm staying," I said.

"Are you out of your mind?" Louie yelled at me, still jumping and waving his arms.

"I'd be out of my mind to wander around after you and get fried," I yelled back at him. He could not believe his ears. I guess he thought I was just bugging him about the clothes, and he'd taken it for granted that I would go. He stopped jumping.

"You going to stay here and let the buzzards get you?"

My heart took a big fall and started pounding against my chest when he said "buzzards," but I said, "I got more of a chance here than with you and your moon-in-the-right-hand-and-sun-in-the-left-hand shit! Go on! Split! Get the hell out of here! I'm better off without you!"

Louie's expression changed. He looked like a cornered dog, scared and mean. He started toward me slowly.

"Get those clothes, goddamn you!"

"Get them yourself," I said, watching, tensing, getting ready.

"Get those clothes!"

"Screw you!"

Louie came at me with eyes that said one thing—*murder!* If we had been wearing our clothes, we would have had our knives, and we would have cut each other to pieces.

I swung for his eye and felt blood on my knuckles, but he got me on the shoulder. I staggered, and before I could get my balance, he caught me on the side of the head. As I fell, I grabbed his leg and pulled him down. I tried to kick him in the groin, but he had his knee in my belly, his hands on my throat. I thrashed with my legs and tried to pry his thick fingers from my neck, but he squeezed tighter and tighter. I went blind. Frantically, my fingers searched his face and found the hollows under his eyes. I pushed, and he jerked his head back. His fingers loosened from my neck. With one big heave of my body, I threw him off.

I lay on the ground, sick to my stomach, sucking big gulps of air.

Louie sprawled, panting, near me. He pulled himself to his feet and sobbed, "I'm not going to sit on my ass under a rock and starve to death! I gotta move!" He staggered a few steps, and I heard him pause. "You coming?"

"No," I said, and without turning to look at him, I crawled to the cave.

SIX

I woke starving. My stomach made loud noises trying to eat itself up, and it ached from Louie's knees. I had a sore throat from his fingers. But when I turned and stretched my legs in the space I did not have to share—I felt great! I could breathe without choking on my hate. I was rid of Louie! I was free! I could do exactly what I wanted. Now my luck would change.

In a few minutes, I decided, I would hunt for

berries or something to quiet my stomach and tide me over till the chopper came back, probably not till the next day, because I could tell from the light that it was late afternoon. I had no doubt that it would return. I would be ready. I would gather a pile of wood, and then at daybreak I'd light a signal fire and never let it go out. I would make it down the riverbed far enough from the canyon so there would be room for the chopper to sit down.

I got high thinking about the landing! The chopper blades beating the air, shaking the big bush with their wind . . . Pop and Ted hopping out, grinning . . . would they be happy they found me! Would I be glad to see them! They were great people. Pop was a cool old guy, and Ted in his dumb jock way was a neat dude. And Joe and Mike and Ray and even fat, stupid Two-Ton Tony! Salt of the earth, man, salt of the earth!

I wondered where old craphead was. He had left without taking his clothes. Maybe he would die of pneumonia in the desert night. Tough.

But suddenly in my mind I saw his little blue eyes, open, dead, staring at the million lights hanging in the black sky without seeing them, the buzzards circling lower and lower. . . . I got the hell out of the cave, my heart pounding.

The sandy hill opposite, now in shadow but bright from the reflected glare of the desert, faced me—a blank wall sprouting a few scattered bushes. To my left the canyon, climbing the high hill, narrowed to a gash near the top. I saw nothing on that low, bare mountain that cared if I lived or died.

I turned and looked down-canyon. The big bush blocked my view, but beyond it two buzzards gliding in circles caught the late-afternoon sunlight. High as they were, they could see for miles. The bushes, the hills, the canyons, the dry riverbeds—maybe even the campground with the people making their evening meal. They did not give a damn. They were looking for dinner— dead flesh.

Suddenly I thought, suppose Louie makes it and I don't? *I should have gone with Louie.* That s.o.b. would live, and I would die—with no one to know except the buzzards. . . . How could I have been so sure the chopper would return to this very spot . . . and me less than a dot in the great empty. . . .

Night was coming!

I panicked. I needed fire more than I needed food. I needed a roaring fire to push away the dark, to dim the lights hanging in the black sky! I spotted a couple of twisty, weedy gray branches on the ground across the gully, and I bounded toward them. A rock rolled under my foot. I sprawled on my stomach on the stony bed of the gully, and a sharp pain stabbed my left leg from ankle to knee.

What if I had broken my leg?

Carefully I got to my feet and put the weight on my left leg. I almost sobbed in relief when I found I could stand on it. Then I felt the smart of a scraped, bleeding elbow. What if I fell another time and broke a leg, an arm, cracked my skull? My head ached, my throat ached, my stomach ached. Maybe I was sick . . . suppose I died with only the buzzards to know?

"HELP!" I screamed. "HELP, GODDAMN IT, HELP!"

"What's wrong? What is it?" Louie appeared from behind the big bush. He hadn't left me! I could have kissed him. We ran to each other. I wondered if I looked as bad as he did. His left eye was almost closed by a purple puffiness cracked by a bloody split. The other eye was wide open in fear.

But even as I ran toward him I remembered how I hated him. He would pay for being such a bastard, a Big Man who chewed his fingernails; pay for my terror, for every lousy thing that was wrong.

"What is it, man?" he asked anxiously.

"A rattlesnake this long!" I held my arms open wide.

"I'm leaving!" He took a few steps away from me, then he turned back. Tears ran down his cheeks, making paths through the dirt. "Is it still there?" His voice shook so he could hardly talk.

"Not in the cave, you creep."

"Where?" Louie looked around him wildly.

"Shit, man, he went away. He rolled away like a hoop, throwing kisses with his tail! You can stop bawling, chickie!"

Still blubbering, Louie cursed me and made a wide detour around me. Cautiously he approached the shallow cave, dropping to his hands and knees, peering inside, trying to get up nerve to crawl into it for his clothes. Several times he shot out his arm and drew it back. I laughed at him.

"I can't do it, Dave—" He looked at me, begging. "Please. I'm cold."

I loved it. "Times are tough all over," I said, turning my back on him.

The desert, gold color in the late-afternoon light, rolled away from the canyon like a big rug dotted with bushes, covering hills, sinking into hollows. Along the eastern edge, the low, far mountains were pale red, and over it all the sky was light, cloudless blue. Yesterday this time I was sitting down to eat with the other guys. Only twenty-four hours? It seemed more like twenty-four days.

I was getting cold myself, and I went to the cave for my clothes. Louie sat chewing his nails, huddled to keep warm, in the gully nearby. I took his knife out of his jeans and threw his clothes at him as if I was throwing a dog a bone. I got into my own jeans and shirt while he shook each piece of clothing thoroughly to make sure no rattler hid in it. He did not look at me.

I sat down again beside the big bush, looking out over the desert for smoke from campfires, town lights, anything that might show up now that the sun had set. Louie approached me timidly.

"I'm starving."

"Yessir. What will it be, sir, a couple hamburgers or a steak? Well-done or rare?"

"Go to hell!" Louie sat with his back to me, but I knew what he was doing.

"Too bad you don't have salt. They'd taste better." Louie gave no sign that he heard me, but when I stood up and began gathering rocks, he quickly joined me.

Without speaking, without looking at each other, we wandered around searching for rabbits, squirrels, birds. I would have considered rats, I was so hungry. But the only game in sight was a few birds who would not let us near enough for good aim, and we missed them by miles. A half hour later when I stopped hunting animals and turned to the plants, Louie was right there with me, gnawing and sucking his fingers, watching my every move. The creep had no ideas of his own, but he made sure I would not find anything he did not know about.

I went to the big bush in the middle of the gully. It was a real mother, the heavy lower branches spreading about twelve, fifteen feet from outside tip to outside tip. They were bigger than my thigh where they curved out of the thick trunk, a foot, a foot and a half off the ground. They tapered to twig thickness at the ends. Smaller branches curved up from those and smaller ones from *those,* carrying hundreds of bright red twigs with pairs of tiny, narrow dark green leaves.

And among the twigs and leaves hung clusters of deep purple berries the size of cherry pits!

I crammed a handful into my mouth—and so did Louie. They were mostly white inside, slightly bitter, but not terrible. I could have put up with the taste, but they were too woody, too splintery, and we both choked trying to swallow them. We had to spit them out.

There were bushes and small trees and cactus everywhere and many plants less than an inch high, each one sitting in a small piece of vacant land. The trees and bushes grew low and scraggly, and their leaves, mostly gray and dusty, were always small. And almost always the plants lived with death, living stalks and stems and roots growing out of bleached, weedy skeletons.

I chewed every kind of leaf I saw. Louie copied me, after waiting to see if I would drop dead. Nothing tasted really *bad,* but everything was dry, and we just did not have enough spit to get it down. Up the canyon a fluffy, shapeless tree carried a million small yellow flowers. I tried them, but they were not juicy enough, either.

"There has to be *something* for us to eat!" Louie burst out, wiping a shred of yellow flower from his lip. "How did the Indians make it?"

I was too depressed and too tired to chop him. I said, "All I know is what I've seen in the flicks. Indian stalks deer. Deer raises head. Indian aims arrow and lets go of bowstring. Indian has dinner."

"Yeh, I know that number. And the one about the dude lost in the desert, staggering around, dying of thirst. And when he's just about wiped out, he finds this beautiful little puddle and flops on his belly and drinks and drinks! And then they find him! Man, I need a drink of water! I need something to eat!"

While we were looking for dinner, the sky had gone through light blue, dark blue, and now it was black again. Louie looked back up the canyon. Over our heads the moon was high, round as a baseball, like a weak searchlight. In the north we could see a bank of clouds dimly lighted, like a threat. Louie turned to me.

"How long does it take to starve to death?"

SEVEN

"Let's get some wood and make a fire," I said. "That way we can keep warm at night, cook if we get anything to cook, and the smoke will be a signal when the chopper comes back tomorrow."

"That chopper isn't coming back. We have to walk out ourselves."

"You're crazy, man!" I said, hanging on to my panic. "They'll search until they find us."

"Why? What's in it for them?"

"What do you mean, what's in it for them? We're lost. They *have* to search for us!"

"O.K., so they searched. They did their duty. Who do you think you are, a friend of the governor?" Louie's mouth twisted in a sneer.

"Go to hell!" My panic got away from me, and I flew into a rage, but I knew I could not take another fight. I jumped to my feet as much to get away as for any other reason.

"You go that way and look for wood, I'll look over here," I said, but Louie stuck to me like glue. He was at my elbow as we crossed and recrossed the gully and went down the riverbed. There was not much wood to be gathered, only skinny boughs and runners and an occasional chunk of dried root. It took us an hour or so in the dark even to gather a small pile. We decided to wait till morning to hunt for more.

You would think that on a desert it would be easy to start a fire, that dry branches and twigs would burn like paper. You would be wrong.

First of all, a nasty cold wind came up and gave us trouble. Even when Louie cupped his hands and I held the match till my fingers were burned, the wood did not catch. Louie took over, fishing his matchbook out of his pocket.

"I set our house on fire once and they had to call the fire department," he said as he lighted the first match and I cupped my hands. He did no better than I had.

"Damn, I can't start a fire without paper or old rags!" He took off a sock, held the match to it, and dropped it on the woodpile. Without ever flaming, the burning edge ate the sock, leaving ash, and the wood never caught.

"How did Pop do it, besides talking to it?" Louie asked.

"He made a little tepee out of small sticks and got that started," I said, and remembering, I leaned twigs against each other and started lighting matches again. A couple times I got a twig the size of a toothpick to burn, but when it reached a big piece of wood, it went out as if it was turned off.

"Let's save the rest of our matches till daylight, so we can see what we're doing," I said.

"I'm splitting as soon as it gets light. I'm not going to hang around here. You better come with me!"

"No way."

"Then stay here and feed the buzzards! I'm leaving!"

"Screw you!" I punched Louie on the arm and ran to the cave. My cave, my home sweet home.

Some home! That hunk of rock did not put out one degree of heat. My teeth chattered, and I rolled myself in a ball and hugged myself, but I still shivered. Cold and miserable as I was, I would not leave this cave, where at least I had protection from the glare of day and the dark of night. And it was a definite place, a cave made by a boulder at the foot of a hill. It was like having an address, much better than one bush after another under an open sky, which was nowhere at all.

But what would I do if Louie split in the morning?

When I was a little kid I used to have nightmares that I was lost, and I would wake up yelling, "Ma-ma, I want my ma-ma!" That was how I felt now as I lay shivering and chattering, my stomach aching, my head aching, my throat aching from Louie's fingers.

He crawled in beside me. He was shivering, and his teeth were chattering, too. We sat as close as we could, but we did not speak. I hated him with a hot hate for my bruised stomach and neck, for being cold and hungry, for being in this freezing cave, for being a lousy Barber. I hated him so much I felt I would blow up like a bomb.

And I felt his hate reaching out to me. Like two crackling currents, his hate and mine passed back and forth between us. Outside the overhang the cold wind blew stronger every minute. Without thinking, we moved closer together and Louie put his arm around my shoulder. We sat in the freezing darkness of the cave, starving, hugging each other, hating each other.

We fell asleep.

EIGHT

I woke up when Louie took his arm from my shoulders. The wind howled down the canyon and screamed and sucked around the boulder.

"I'm freezing," he said. Then he crawled away and ducked his head out beyond the overhang. "Man, look at those clouds!"

I crawled to his side and leaned out. The cloud bank had become a high, puffy wall that raced toward us from the north and, as we watched, covered the moon. The cold wind cut right through my empty stomach and pelted my face with sand and bits of rock. I quickly moved back into the cave, and Louie followed me. We shivered in silence, as close to each other as we could press.

"I wonder if they ever found the jeep," Louie said in a shaky voice.

"Probably. That thing would show up like a red craphouse."

"It should have pulled us out with no strain. That's what those jeeps are made for. I wonder what I did to it."

"Whatever you did, you did it good!"

"Ted thinks every inch of that car is holy."

"I know," I said. "You're in trouble, man, and I'm right there with you."

I hadn't considered till now what we had to face when we got back (*if* we got back, but I put the *if* out of my mind). How bad had Louie wrecked the car? What if they hadn't found it at all? Look what trouble that son-of-a-bitch had got me into!

Louie rested his head on his knees. His shoulders drooped. "I really blew it this time . . . so what's new." I knew he was chewing his fingers. Then he said, "I can't take much more of this. If they don't find us tomorrow, I'll be wiped out."

"Stop feeling sorry for yourself, craphead. You'll make it. You're too rotten to die. And they'll find us, and they'll bust us!" I took my arm from his shoulder and jabbed him with my elbow.

What would I do if Louie died? I would be all alone with his corpse and the buzzards . . . and the million lights in the black night. . . .

I put my arm around his shoulders because I was cold, and if he died, I would have no warmth. I had to keep him alive so I could live. We sat close, curled up as tightly as possible, our heads hunched over our knees. The wind continued to scream and howl down the canyon, to suck out the air in sudden gasps, to blow gusts of sand into the cave. We had to cover our faces.

Suddenly we heard the first spatter of rain. We

scrambled out into the wind. The moon and all the stars had disappeared, but it was still quite light, maybe from the full moon behind the clouds. The sound of raindrops hitting the sand and rocks like hammers filled the canyon. I turned my face up to the sky, my mouth open. Louie stood next to me, his head tipped back, also. We were having the first water we had tasted in over twenty-four hours. It fell on our shoulders, our clothing, and some sweet, sweet drops fell on our dry, stale tongues. The drops came faster and faster until they were streams, as if someone had turned on a cold shower. My hair was plastered to my head; my jeans, my shirt, drenched.

We dove into the cave. We sat soaked and chattering, listening to the steady drumming roar. Water dripped off the overhang and gurgled and clicked as it flowed past. Suddenly we were sitting in two inches of water. I could not believe it. It swept into the cave, pushing hard against me.

"We gotta get out!" I yelled, and we crawled out. The water was running fast down the canyon, and before I realized, it was up to my knees. We stood by the cave in the darkness, hanging on to each other, trying to keep our balance in the sand that was being washed away from under our shoes, and against the force of the water pushing us and slamming rocks and pieces of bushes into us. We heard sounds like thunderclaps as the rocks hit the boulder and each other. Then one of them hit me in the back and I went down.

I could not get up. The sand slipped away under my hands and slid from beneath my feet. The water fought me, slapped me, pushed me, ran into my nostrils. I could not raise my head high enough to breathe air. I thought, *This is crazy, drowning in the desert!* The more I struggled to get up, the more water poured into my lungs. A hand grabbed my arm, let go, found my hair. I couldn't breathe. . . . I stopped struggling.

I came to, coughing and fighting for breath. Louie was pounding me, shaking me, slapping my face. I dimly saw him, a dark form, bending over me. The rain drummed, and I heard the flood rushing past, but I was not in it. "I'm cold," I whimpered, "I'm cold!"

"Dave!" Louie yelled, and he rubbed and pinched and punched.

Still I cried, "I'm cold, I'm cold!"

Finally he collapsed on top of me, panting and sobbing. "Dave, I'm wiped out. I can't do any more for you. . . . Don't die, man! For God's sake, don't die on me!"

I shivered and whimpered for a while under his dead, wet weight. Then his warmth entered into me, and I fell asleep.

NINE

I opened my eyes. My head ached where Louie had grabbed my hair. He was still lying on me like a ton of bricks. At first I thought he was dead, but he was warm, and his warmth kept me warm. The parts of me that escaped from under his sprawl were freezing cold and clammy wet.

I turned my head. It was morning. The rain had stopped, and the world was the color of winter. The sky, the broken clouds, the desert, the light that filled the spaces in between were steel gray. The bushes stood black and still and tough, each in its own territory.

Louie stirred and rolled off me. I curled up to save his warmth. Lying on my side, I saw we were on a mound two, three feet above the floor of the gully. Where the flood ran an hour or two ago, now there was wet sand with threads of water winding from side to side, combining, separating, coming together, always running downhill. The force of the flood had widened and deepened the gully, slicing its sides off sharp and extending it so far into the dry riverbed I could not see where it ended. The overhang that made our cave was now high enough from the ground so that Louie and I would be able to stand in it.

I shifted my shoulders and realized we were by the big bush in the canyon. What a tough mother! Yesterday it had been growing a foot or so above the gully floor. Today it was on a mound about three feet above the wet, sandy streambed, with rocks heaped against it on the uphill side. The flood had swept those rocks—a couple the size of watermelons—and slammed them against the soil held by the roots snaking out from the fat, short base of the bush. Those roots held the rocky soil like in a fist and forced the flood to go around the plant's territory.

Louie sat up and coughed. "I'm freezing," he said, hugging himself to keep warm. "Man! What a night! You felt like cold, wet rubber, Dave!" He stood up and stamped his feet and flung his arms around. "Man, I really thought you were dead!"

I looked at him with his shiner and his hair like a bird's nest, chattering, shivering, stamping, and I thought to myself, That ugly craphead saved my life!

"Hey, Louie, thanks," I said. He did not answer, just went on hitting himself and jumping around.

I stayed rolled into a ball on the ground and shook and watched the sky beyond the faraway mountains turn milky orange while the clouds got brighter and brighter. Then the sun jumped those mountains and climbed up the sky. The higher it climbed, the stronger it got, lighting the plants into sparkles, forcing its heat through my wet clothes to touch my freezing, clammy body.

Louie stopped hopping around and stripped, then dropped to the ground. His muscles relaxed, his face lost its tenseness as his cold, wet flesh toasted in the strong sun. I struggled out of my own clothing and collapsed on the mound, and my flesh warmed, my blood began to move, my life returned. I slept and dreamed about a double cheeseburger on a clean white plate sitting near my head under the bush. I could even smell it.

When I woke up, instead of the cheeseburger I saw my wet clothes bunched and crumpled under the bush. It occurred to me that we would need those clothes when the sun went down. I pulled myself up. I was stronger in spite of my starvation. I started to spread my jeans and shirt and underwear, bright and clean from the rain and flood, on the stiff twigs and upcurving branches.

"Hey, Louie, spread your clothes so they'll dry."

"You my mother?"

"You'll need dry clothes when it gets cold."

"Go to hell!" He did not even open his eyes.

I spread his clothes on the other side of the bush from mine, because he had saved my life, but that was all I would do for him. He'd gotten me into this mess in the first place. Because of him the last sight my eyes would see would be this big, bush-dotted vacant lot. I knew I couldn't live forever, but I hadn't figured on dying this week, either. . . .

Then my legs buckled under me, and I dropped to the ground near the bush and cried like a little kid. After a while I thought, Maybe I'm dreaming, and I uncovered my face. . . . No, it was true. I was trapped in the middle of miles and miles of bushes and rocks and sand.

Except that now the ground was bright from the rain, dotted with tiny, blooming flowers. The bushes were greener; tall, thorny whips I had not noticed before held up orange-red flowers like torches eight, ten feet off the ground. The mountains at the edge of the desert were so close I could see every fold, every wrinkle. Puffy

clouds filled with light sailed across the sky. And
at my back the barrel trunk of the big bush held
the tapering, upcurved branches and millions of
twigs spread out to catch the sun and sparkle like
daytime stars!

But for Louie and me the buzzards slid in silent circles on the air, now low enough for me to
see the individual rounded feathers at the ends
of their wings. Only they would know what happened to me, because no one else was here . . .
not my mom, blaming herself as usual for everything that is wrong with my life . . . not Jack, my
stepfather (I would have taken ten beatings to see
his scowling face at that moment) . . . not my
brothers or sisters or the guys I used to run
around with, or my best friend, Mac . . . Debbie,
my Rancho Verde lady, wasn't here to wrap herself around me and make me forget I was going
to die.

Only the buzzards were here. . . .

And Louie.

If I spoke, he would hear me. If I put out my
hand, I could touch him. He'd brought me to my

death, but he was here when I needed him most. He was all I had. I moved close to him.

"Thanks again for saving my life," I said in a shaky voice, "even if it is only for a couple of days. . . ."

Louie turned toward me, his face pinched and tired and dirty, his lips trembling, but his good eye sending me a message of hate.

"Shove it! What good are you to me? I almost killed myself keeping you alive. For what? To rot out here for the buzzards?"

"Louie, Louie, I'm all you've got!" I said, holding my hand out to him.

He ignored it. "Now it's too late. We should've walked back yesterday!" He pounded the ground with his fist. "Ever since I was born the whole world has been screwin' me. No matter what I do, I can't win!"

"Come on, man, don't talk like that. It's not over—yet."

"B.S. I'm a loser and you're another!"

"You're not a loser! You're a goddamn hero! You saved my life!"

Louie laughed. "Big deal. I'd rather be the sorriest loser and alive than the biggest hero and dead!"

The last thing I needed right now was his hate. "Forget it," I said, turning my back on him. . . . What a lonely thing it would be to die out here with nobody to know about the most important night in our lives, the night when Louie was a hero, the night I almost drowned.

"*Dave!*" Louie was crawling toward me, reaching for me. The shiner, the messed-up hair, the dirt on his face were the same as they had been a second before, but he was no longer Ugly Louie. He was a guy as lonely and scared as I was. I grabbed his hand. "What the hell are we going to do, Dave?" he sobbed.

"I don't know." I threw my arm around his neck. I had the feeling that as long as I could see him and hear him and touch him, I had a chance.

"I don't want to die! I'm too young! My luck might change!"

"Yeh. Things can get better, but when you're dead, that's it. No more maybe, no more nothin'!" Clinging to Louie, I looked out over the desert, desperately searching for a lifesaver. The gully suddenly beckoned and promised. "I wonder what would happen if we followed the creek," I said.

I could see the idea take hold. Louie wiped his face with the back of his hand. We got to our feet and stood side by side staring down the widened, still-damp streambed.

"Probably crosses a road somewhere," he said.

"What have we got to lose?" I asked.

Out of force of habit, or maybe because we were getting ready to leave, we took a long last look at the scene we had been scanning every few minutes since yesterday afternoon. Except for our little mountain, a solid, sandy, rocky wall at our backs (gashed by the gully, of course) and the mountains miles and miles away on the horizon, now bleaching and shrinking in the morning sun, there was nothing. Only millions of sparkling bushes and scrubby trees moving their branches gently.

Louie let out a roar. He had been looking in a

different direction, and he jumped into the air as if he'd gotten a ten-thousand-volt jolt. I could not make out what he was bawling, but when I followed his outstretched arm, I saw a little red square, rocking and dipping among the bushes.

"IT'S THE JEEP!"

We jumped up and down and yelled and waved our arms. The jeep disappeared.

"Let's go!" Louie headed out into the desert.

"Wait!"

He stopped in his tracks. I said, "They're moving, and you're moving! You'll never find 'em!" I ran to him and grabbed his hand. "Stay here!"

He jerked his hand away, yelling, "How will they find us? How will they know we're here?"

We faced each other, each afraid the other was right.

"Oh, God, don't let them go away! Please make them see us!" I prayed as I ran from one place to another to get a better look.

"They'll get away!" Louie bawled hoarsely, wringing his hands. "They'll go away!"

And he took off among the bushes like a

broken field runner. I took off after him.

Suddenly the jeep poked its square hood over the top of a rise we had not even known was there. It was so close I could make out two figures inside.

TEN

"Hey! Over here! Over here!" Louie yelled, streaking away in a sprint. I was right beside him, hollering and waving my arms.

"Over here! Over here!" we yelled, waving frantically, trying to head off the now-dusty jeep as it zigzagged around rocks and bushes to enter the riverbed and turn toward us. We met it a couple hundred feet downstream from the bush.

Pop exploded from the passenger's side.

"We found 'em! We found 'em!" he yelled. "I knew we'd find 'em! Oh, thank God we found 'em!" He grabbed each of us in a bear hug, his face split in two with grinning and laughing. Ted did not get out of the jeep.

"Hi, Ted!" I yelled.

"Hey, Ted, I didn't wreck the jeep!" Louie yelled at the same time. Ted did not answer either of us.

Pop would not stop pounding us and hugging us. "Did you see those sons of guns run? How did you get the shiner, Louie? Look at your neck, Dave! Didn't you guys have enough to worry about without fighting? . . . They look like hell, but they're in great shape!"

"What do you mean, great shape?" I yelled, laughing like an idiot. "We're starving, and we almost froze to death, and I almost drowned!"

"We're starving and he almost drowned!" Louie echoed, laughing and crying.

"He saved me from drowning!" I yelled.

"—a brilliant idea using your clothes as an

SOS!" Pop yelled, talking at the same time. We kept yelling at each other as if we were half a mile away. "Those jazzy shirts and white underwear showed up in my binoculars like a billboard! Where were you yesterday? We were all over this area!"

"I see the jeep's O.K.," Louie yelled again. Ted sat behind the wheel as if he was stone deaf.

We ran to the bush and got into our damp jeans and gathered the rest of our clothing.

"Ted's mad," I said to Louie.

"I know," Louie said.

Pop had followed us, and he stood looking at the bush. "I see you found your elephant tree, Dave," he said. "That's the biggest one I have ever seen."

I reared back and stared at the tangle of boughs and twigs and tiny leaves sparkling in the sun. Near me a little branch had broken in the storm, and a red trickle oozed down the rough, reddish bark. It did look like blood, but it smelled like plants.

"I wouldn't be surprised if it's maybe a

hundred and fifty years old," Pop said.

A hundred and fifty years of squatting in the sun, fighting wind, fighting flood. . . . A bush you would pass right by and never see . . . and Louie and I, who figured we were so tough, wouldn't have lasted a week.

"See how the branches curve up like elephants' trunks raised to trumpet?"

The idea seemed pretty far out to me, but elephants' trunks or not, that was one hell of a bush. A hundred-and-fifty-year-old brute that saved my life and Louie's. And you could pass it by and never notice.

Ted had driven almost up to us, and we climbed into the jeep. He backed down the wash until it was wide enough for him to turn, then we crawled over a bank and started cross-country.

I looked out the back window. The elephant tree squatted on its mound doing exactly what it had been doing every single day for one hundred and fifty years. . . . The fat barrel trunk drew power from the earth for the explosion of branches and twigs and leaves glistening in the sun. *It was surviving!*

We made a slight turn, and the elephant tree faded into the sandy cut. We turned still more, and the cut disappeared as if the two sides of the hill had come together and closed the canyon. As far as I was concerned the world of the gully had come to an end.

Louie and I faced each other on the little seats as we had on Monday coming to the desert. Pop sat half-turned so he could talk to us, his face still almost split from ear to ear, grinning.

"Why didn't you hang your clothes on the elephant tree yesterday? We would have picked you up then."

"Because they weren't wet," we said, and we told him about the flood.

"You poor bastards," he said, turning to Ted. "They had it rough." Ted said nothing, but his neck got red. He didn't say a word all the time we told what happened to us. He drove with tender, loving care, avoiding boulders, carefully crawling over rises, dipping into hollows, slowly hobbling over ruts and plowing through sand.

Finally Louie asked, "When did you find the jeep? I guess I didn't wreck it, did I, Ted?"

Pop told us they thought we had split back to town and they'd gone after us in the station wagon till they got to the junction with the main highway. They asked the guy at the gas station if we had passed and he said no, so they came back and took the same jeep road we had. They found the car right away, probably not long after we had left it. It turned out we had not gone very far from camp, and that the jeep was pretty close to the road, not miles away as it had seemed.

"What was wrong with it?" Louie asked, chewing his little finger.

"You didn't have it in four-wheel-drive," Pop said. "You fellas are going to have to deal with Ted, you know. You caused a lot of trouble!" He tried to be serious, but his eyes were shining, and his mouth turned up at the corners. At least Pop is on our side, I thought to myself.

Suddenly we were rolling along on the jeep road, and then we were back in camp. Just half an hour from a cave in the great big empty to the rest of the world! Food! People! A hot shower! Heaven!

ELEVEN

I slept for hours. My stomach woke me, growling the way it had growled in the cave the day before. For a few sweet seconds I stretched out in my sleeping bag the way I had stretched out in the cave, but this time I smelled onion and garlic cooking, heard the guys messing around. The sound of their voices was like music. Salt of the earth, those guys—Mike, Ray, Joe, even Two-Ton Tony in his own fat, stupid way. And Pop, almost crying, he was so glad to find us . . . such a sweet old guy. . . .

Ted.

He had not smiled once. He was not glad we hadn't died. That figured. He would never be lost in his whole life. That son-of-a-bitch would always know exactly where he was and stride on those thick jock legs of his to wherever he wanted to go. Or better yet, he would ride in the high, square, bright red jeep with the hooded lights, the winch, all the other goodies . . . not even five hundred miles on the speedometer . . . its tires still clean, the new-car smell strong. And Ted stroking it, loving it. And then it was gone. Ripped off by two crapheads who could have totaled it without even trying. . . . And *he* had to drive all over the desert looking for them, and when they were found they came running and jumping like a couple of kids on a school playground. No wonder he was sour.

I wanted to tell Louie what I had been thinking. Maybe we should apologize. Maybe we should try to tell Ted . . . what?

99

I got up, dressed, and crawled out of the tent. It was late afternoon. The desert surrounding the campground was colored gold as it had been the day before when I looked across its distances from the elephant tree, when I was starving and lonely and scared. Pop was at the fire pit stirring a stew. A healthy active fire jumped against the bottom of the coffeepot. I wished I had seen him start it. Ted and the jeep were gone.

Louie was with the other guys. His face kind of lighted up when he saw me, and his good eye crinkled in a smile.

"Hey, man," he said.

"Wow! Look at the marks on his neck!" Mike held out his hand to Joe. "You owe me. Louie killed him!"

"You're crazy! Look at your guy's face! Look at the eye!" Joe said.

Louie and I ignored them. We stood side by side, and I said to him, "Did you find out—is Ted going to bust us?"

"I don't give a damn. They'll just put us on probation." But he gnawed at his thumb.

"Good thing you weren't found Tuesday night." Ray grinned at us like a black alligator. "Ted would've torn you dudes apart, both of you at the same time. He was *mad!*"

"He cooled down last night when it rained, but since you guys are back he's really ticked off again. He says he's going to beat the crap out of both of you," Mike said.

Nobody seemed to care much that we almost died. . . .

The smell of onions and garlic crawled into my nose. I looked over to where Pop stirred the stew bubbling in the pot.

"I'll worry about that later," I said, and I hung my arm around Louie's neck. "This sure beats the cave, right?"

"Right! Dig that smell, man! Look at that fire!"

"Can you believe those dudes?" Ray shook his head.

"What do you want us to do, kill each other?" Louie glared at Ray.

"He saved my life!" I said to them. "I would have drowned!"

"Well, hell, man, you were better than nothing," Louie said. I popped him on the arm.

Two-Ton Tony had been watching us from behind his fat cheeks, looking from one guy to the other. He opened his mouth, and a high, girlish voice came out.

"When did you boys make up?" he chirped.

For a split second there was a stunned silence, then everybody landed on Tony, pounding him as if he were a drum, yelling like idiots. "It talks! It talks!"

"It's a girl!"

"No, it's a fruitcake!"

"I thought it was deaf and dumb!" I yelled to Louie.

"You're only half wrong, it's not deaf!" Louie yelled back.

Pop came over and began yanking guys away and hollering for us to knock it off. Tony struggled free and ran away, but as usual he stayed close enough so that he would not miss anything. Just then Ted drove up, and Pop said chow was on. Louie and I sprinted to the table and sat down next to each other.

That was the best time of the whole day. The stew, an enormous pot of it, smelling like heaven in the middle of the table. French bread, and pickles and tomatoes, and coffee with a perfume better than roses. . . . And all around us people laughing and talking and going to get water, to the Ranger's office, to the john, to their tents and campers . . . and other people driving their cars and sputtering their motorbikes . . . coming, going. . . . And beyond the lights and sounds of the camp, the big, bush-dotted empty spread to the edges of the sky. It was still pink, bright day in the west, but in the east night was coming— fast and dark.

And Louie and I were found!

But gradually the good feeling wore off. Ted sat at the end of the table turned half away from the rest of us, silently putting away food, staring at the darkening desert as if the noisy camp-ground or the guys at the table did not exist. He made me uneasy.

But more than that. The other guys were our

own kind. I had thought they would want to know how we had survived, even if he didn't.

I wanted to tell them how great it had felt to be found when we were sure we were going to die. Pop started us off right.

"Tell us from the beginning everything that happened," he said.

So Louie and I told them almost everything—the mirage, the chopper, the flood. More and more we talked to each other, living the whole trip together, all of it, including the parts we didn't tell—the dark night, the bad dreams, the fights.

"You fellas had a tough go," Pop said, looking at Ted, who stared out over the desert, giving no sign he heard.

Then the guys started asking the wrong questions.

"Did you dudes fight right away?" Mike asked.

"Did you settle it the first time?" Ray asked.

"We won, didn't we, Davy baby?" Joe said.

"He hardly touched me," Louie said with his old sneer.

"Look at that shiner!" Joe said. "Some touch!"

"What did you fellas have against each other?" asked Pop.

"They had a difference of opinion." Mike smirked. "Louie thought Dave was a garbage pig, and Dave did not agree."

Everyone laughed. Louie and I sat side by side filling our bellies with Pop's good stew, not looking at each other, not talking. I wished they would all drop dead. My old everyday self was returning, and I didn't want it. Not yet. I didn't want to fight the whole world again so soon after I almost lost it.

"No, seriously, you fellas never saw each other before Monday," Pop said. "How about it, Louie? Dave?"

"We're people, people fight," Louie mumbled into his plate.

"Don't give me that tired old stuff," Pop said.

Mike said, "Look at the wars. My old man was in three of them, killed in the last one. Read the papers, man, watch the news."

"Cop out," Pop said. "Talk about the whole

world and all the wars, and you don't have to talk about yourselves. Meantime, some poor kid gets cut up or shot for no good reason!"

Pop's remark reminded the guys of something. Four pairs of eyes asked us the same question. Tony's fork stopped halfway to his mouth, and he piped in his womanish voice, "Why didn't you use the knives?" Ray, who sat next to him, slammed him on the arm. He dropped his fork, shielded his head with his arms, and frantically squirmed and twisted and tried to hoist his elephant legs over the bench to run away.

Pop flipped out. This was the first he knew about the blades. "Knives!" he exploded. "You damn fools! Hand them over—*now!*" He would not be put off—no way.

The guys were watching us. Even Tony, who had got one big leg over the bench, stopped trying to escape. In the pocket of my jeans were the two blades where I had put them after the big fight. Next to me Louie sat frozen, waiting to be humiliated and not knowing what to do about it.

106

"They're in our tents," I said to Pop, rising and climbing over the bench. "Come on," I said to Louie. He let his breath out in a big sigh and scrambled after me. As we walked together, I slipped him his knife, and we went to our separate tents.

I returned to the table, handed Pop my blade, and walked over to the fire. The other guys were assuring Pop that nobody else had brought a blade. "I'd hate to have to make a search every time we go on a trip," he told them.

I looked into the jumping, crouching, crackling flames. The fire had become more important, more brilliant as the light faded from the sky . . . orange, red, yellow; flash of blue, touch of green. . . . The most beautiful thing in the world on a cold, dark night is—fire!

And a friend.

"Louie, last night this time, remember?"

"Yeh. We were starving, and no one else was there!" he said to me from the table, where he had just given Pop his knife. He poured us each a mug of coffee and came over to the fire with me.

"Remember putting the match to your sock, trying to get the wood to burn?" I said to him. Last night (only last night?) Louie had been a dim shape in the dark except when the flare of the match showed his bird's-nest hair, his dirty, puffy face. Tonight his hair lay smooth on his head, and his face was clean. Only the puffiness and dark purple of his eye connected the two faces.

He was saying, "Yeh, and the rain. Man, I thought you were dead! You felt like cold, wet rubber!"

Pop was doing his own remembering. "You are looking at a stupid, damn fool," he said. "I was so sure you guys couldn't have gone that far, so sure we would find you any minute . . . and the day passed, and then that storm last night. . . . I couldn't sleep, and as soon as it got light I said to Ted, 'Just one more look, and then I'll have to report to the Ranger and call their folks.' Man, I could be in terrible trouble, right this minute. . . ." For a second his face was lined, tired, then the ear-to-ear grin returned, and he told for the sixth time how, *pow!*, our plaid shirts and white underwear hit him in the eye as he scanned the desert through his binoculars.

"You fellas are geniuses, finding the biggest elephant tree around and using it to hang your clothes on!"

"*Geniuses my ass!* Out of sheer decency I have kept my mouth shut, but *geniuses*, that's too much!" Ted finally acknowledged our existence. He had jumped up by his end of the table and faced us, half-crouched, hands clenched, eyes big and dark and deep-set. "They steal a six-thousand-dollar car and wreck the trip for everybody, and they're treated like heroes. What kind of a deal is that?" His voice rasped like a file.

"Ted, nobody is trying to get them off the hook," Pop said. "We're just glad they're found. They are going to have to settle with you, though, and I suppose now is as good a time as any." He did not sound enthusiastic.

"You bet your goddamn life they're going to settle. They took my car! That's grand theft auto. That's a felony. Hear that, punks? A felony!"

I felt sick to my stomach, and I began to shake

109

the way I had the night before when the wind blew and we were freezing. I raised my mug to my lips, and the coffee slopped out over the rim.

"Don't you think car theft is a little strong, Ted? Actually, they didn't go far, and they didn't put a scratch on your jeep." Pop kept his voice soft and silky.

"We were just going to take a little ride and come right back," Louie said. He sounded false as hell to me.

"—a brand-new six-thousand-dollar car and almost totaled it against a boulder. How come you missed, punk?"

"Ted! I know how you feel—" I began, but I sounded as false as Louie.

"—made a fool out of me in front of everybody! Why? What did I ever do to you punks?" He took a couple steps toward us, and his fists looked like sledgehammers at the ends of his arms.

"Nothing. That's why we're sorry," I said, my voice quavering.

"I'm sorry," Louie said, and I knew he meant it. He really did.

But Ted only laughed. "You know what you can do with your apologies. When I finish with you punks, you'll *know* how sorry you are!" He advanced toward us, head down, face pale, eyes like death, those two sledgehammers lifted a little. The other guys moved restlessly, and a little buzz rose from them. I wondered if they were laying bets, or if they would come in and help us.

Pop quickly climbed over the table bench and planted himself between Ted and us. "Get hold of yourself, Ted," he said in an icy voice, quickly in command. Ted paused uncertainly. At that moment Two-Ton Tony's clear soprano cut across all the other sounds of the campground and the desert night.

"Are you boys more scared now than you were when you were lost?" Then he flung his arms about his head and ducked, but no one hit him. They looked at him, then at Louie and me. I heard myself answering, "No. Out there we were all alone, and we thought we were going to die."

"What did you think about when you thought you were going to die?" Tony leaned on the table toward us. For the first time his eyes were open wide enough for me to see that they were blue, and to see who lived behind them.

"What the hell does this have to do with me?" Ted had lost his momentum, but not his fury. I looked at him squarely—the big blond jock with the clear skin and biceps and calves almost as big as my thighs.

"Ted, do you really think you're ever going to die?" I asked.

He blinked, then made an impatient gesture with one hand. "What kind of stupid question is that?" He lowered his head like a bull. "You threatening me?"

"Oh, no, Ted. . . . But how about this week? What if you're going to die this week?"

I heard Louie catch his breath, and he said, "Yeh, like all of a sudden you're lost, and there's death all around, and you can't believe it, you don't know how it happened—"

"You ripped off my car, that's how it happened!"

Louie ignored him. "—and these two crap-heads kicking and choking and punching each other as if the guy that won would be king of the world . . . but death all around waiting for both of them. . . . All the poor saps had was each other . . . nothing else—"

"I would have drowned," I said.

"—the lonesomeness. Man, that's what gets you—the lonesomeness." Louie's voice trembled, and he gulped his coffee.

I took up where he left off. "You look in every direction a thousand times a day, but there is no one to hear you scream, no one to see you fall . . . only the buzzards. . . . And at night"—I tipped back my head—"at night you look up at the sky . . . all those lights hanging there, maybe a million, and around each one all that black . . . and . . . God Almighty, you realize how big the night is . . . and you think, *what if the earth is lost in space the way Louie and me are lost in the desert. . . ?*"

"And when you come back you realize no one would notice. This whole goddamn earth could fall into the sun and no one would notice till they got their butts singed, because everybody is too busy fighting and screwing each other . . . the damn fools . . . all they have is each other. . . ." Louie's voice trembled, and he stopped talking.

A cold breeze hurried through the camp, creaking guy ropes, flapping tents, whispering to the bushes. Everyone was looking up—Pop, Ted, the other dudes—all of them had their heads tipped back, looking. The night sky suddenly expanded beyond the edges of the desert and arched black and endless beyond the lights hanging overhead. Tony whimpered. Ted let his fists fall.

Louie and I stood shoulder to shoulder, drinking our coffee . . . shivering. . . .

Ted didn't bust us.

Louie and me hang around together.

The guys meet once a week with Pop and Ted.

Hardly anyone misses, which is surprising for a

group of crapheads like us. We talk, we rap, we tell each other there ought to be a better way, but it's tough when the whole world is set up for fighting and everyone screwing the other guy.

Outside of that, we are all pretty much the same. Except that Tony's voice is changing. He talks now.

We've gone on trips to the mountains, to the beach, to a lake for fishing. Next spring we're going back to the desert. Louie and I are going to check on the elephant tree. The other guys want to see it, too. That mother really knows how to survive.